BIKES IN SPACE

Feminist Bicycle Science Fiction

Edited by

ELLY BLUE

Elly Blue Publishing
An imprint of Microcosm Publishing
Portland, Oregon

Bikes in Space, Feminist Bicycle Science Fiction (Volume 1)
© Elly Blue, 2013, 2017
This edition © Microcosm Publishing, 2017

Cover illustration by Katura Reynolds
Fonts by Ian Lynam
All work © its creators, 2013, 2017

First published as *Taking the Lane #10*, 2013, 1,000 copies
Second printing, April 15, 2017, 3,000 copies

Elly Blue Publishing
an imprint of Microcosm Publishing

For a catalog, visit or write:
2752 N Williams Ave.
Portland, OR 97227
TakingTheLane.com
MicrocosmPublishing.com

ISBN 978-1-62106-798-6
This is Microcosm #270

This is the first volume in the Bikes in Space series. To
find other volumes, or to submit your own feminist bicycle
science fiction stories, go to bikesinspace.com

Continue building the Feminist Bicycle Revolution
and find more reading at *TakingTheLane.com* and
MicrocosmPublishing.com

Contents

Introduction

Welcome to the tenth issue of Taking the Lane, and our first go at fiction. It's turned out that switching gears from nonfiction essays to science fiction universes isn't such a far leap. The previous issue, titled "Disaster!" explored ways we are turning to bicycles to rise above cataclysmic events of the past, present, and future; many of the stories here carry the same theme to conclusions as logical as they are fantastical.

Most of the tales in this volume present a bleak view of the future while at the same time managing to be optimistic about the potential of the people living in it to transform it into something better. And it would be hard to come up with a better summation of what this series is all about. Thank you for reading!

Yours from the increasingly distant past,

Elly Blue — Portland, Oregon — March 24, 2013

Spacial Delivery

Maddy Engelfried

The Earth rose over the lunar community of Summerville. Artificial crickets were still chirping and all the windows were dark behind floral-print curtains. No one saw a small figure in a spacesuit step through the hissing airlock. The figure wheeled a bright red Schwinn cruiser at its side. Over its left shoulder it carried a bag of newspapers.

The girl leaned the bike against the inside of the bubble that encased the town and unscrewed her space helmet. Then she peeled off her space suit, stashed it next to the airlock, adjusted her pigtails, slung her bag over her shoulder, and hopped on her bike. She rode into the residential district, past the sign that said:

Welcome to Summerville
The Last Haven of Small Town America.

The stars on the horizon were the same as the ones she had seen on her way to the town, but in a sky that was less black. Summerville was protected by a filter that functioned like a tiny atmosphere, blurring the harshness of space. The artificial sky would begin to turn pink at 5:00 a.m., Earth Eastern Standard Time. By then she would need to be done with her route.

She and her mother had moved to the moon the previous month so that her mother could work at a research station in the next town over. It was still strange looking up at the sky and seeing Earth, and she missed her friends back home. But delivering newspapers wasn't a bad job. The ad on the telescreen had specified that a paperboy was wanted, but once the committee in charge of the town had seen how she could ride, they had hired her immediately. They had even given her the bike, to which she had made a few discreet modifications. They had cautioned her about "maintaining authenticity," but the adjustments were almost invisible to the untrained eye, and anyway no one was awake during her shifts. The most important thing, she reasoned, was that the newspapers got there on time.

She took one hand off the handlebars, reached over her shoulder for a paper, and tossed it into the first yard on the corner. The papers were printed with the same news that flashed on her telescreen every morning, but there were no telescreens in The Last Haven of Small Town America. Her braided pigtails smacked her neck as she whipped around corners, feeling her feet press down on the pedals and squeezing the hand brakes she had installed. She relished the faint breeze on her face and remembered racing through the streets with her friends back on Earth.

This wasn't like home, though, she thought as she pedaled past the malt shop. No robots tended the yards, no sensors blinked from the roofs. There were only white picket fences and window boxes; sometimes a tree, always a pristine green lawn. Grass was expensive on the moon, but this town belonged to people who could afford to live in a bubble of nostalgia for a place and time they had never even known.

Even though no one was around to impress, she practiced tricks, hurling the newspapers over her shoulder and behind her back, turning corners with her hands off the handlebars. She made the papers swish through the middles of tire swings and land squarely on front porches. Her bag lightened, bouncing against the side of her body as she rocketed down the street, tossing papers left and right.

When the bag was empty, she checked the watch her employers had given her. It blinked blue: 4:55 a.m.. Perfect timing. She turned the last corner, back to the airlock where she'd started. There she braked, swung one leg over the side of the bike, leaned it against the bubble, and grabbed her space suit, donning it quickly and stuffing the empty newspaper bag in a pocket. She breezed through the airlock on her bike just as the sky began to change color.

Outside Summerville, she sighed with relief. She was free. There was nothing out here but launchpads and sampling stations, and she still had an hour before school started.

She began to pedal faster, marveling at how little resistance met her feet without the pressure of an artificial atmosphere. In the gray dust she swept wide circles that left tire tracks no wind would erase, cruising in and out of ancient fissures dug by lunar lava, skirting the edges of huge craters and dipping into smaller ones. She hurtled down hills that had once been volcanoes, bouncing over ridges and laughing with delight at how long it took her tires to hit the ground.

This was the best part of living on the moon, the part that made up for the homesickness—biking at one sixth of Earth's gravity against a backdrop of more stars than she'd ever seen on Earth.

It took massive effort, but she waited until Summerville was out of sight before firing up the jet packs.

An Object In Motion

Elizabeth Buchanan

Have you ever dreamed you were falling?

I know, I know—one of *those* questions. It's primal, people say, as if we fell out of enough trees along the evolutionary line that we come preprogrammed with the sound of rushing wind, with the feeling that any second now we're going to hit. I wonder about all those kids growing up in orbit. Do they dream in the same gravity we do, some ancestral gravity? If not, are they human?

But people don't ask those kinds of questions to get into discussions about evolution, and they don't ask them to hear about your dreams, not really. The guy asking if you dream about falling is really just looking for an opening so he can tell you about some crazy dream he had, the one that he's secretly proud of, that he thinks maybe is the sign that he has a creative subconscious. I'm not the kind of girl to subject anybody to my dreams. Still. Sometimes...

Especially this winter, on early mornings like this one when the road is dark almost all the way to work, flat and the same for miles, sometimes I get going fast enough so the wind numbs my ears and drowns out even the cricket hiss of the bike chain underneath me. Those times, when I'm lucky, the words just don't kick in. I don't worry. I don't even think. For a little while, I become something else. An animal of speed and gravity. With the sky pressing down overhead and the asphalt pushing me up to meet it, I am a willing body in the hands of a physical force, shoving and turning and speeding ahead. Keeping me moving. Holding me together. Those mornings—this morning—I get why falling might be something to dream about.

Lights and a honk.

...and in a moment the feeling is gone. I'm here again, just a pantshitting little animal on wheels trying to pull to the far side of the lane before the tankerful of ethanol attached to this pair of headlights grinds me into the dust. He honks again and holds it down. *Asshole.*

I brake and skid off onto the shoulder as the fat black cylinder of the tanker barrels past, spitting gravel as it burns off down the empty road. I reach behind me in my backpack and check my phone. It's five a.m. I sit and watch the taillights until they swerve off onto Eaton Drive, maybe half a mile off, and disappear around the big hill on Hennessey Road, the only bump the terraformers have left in this landscape for miles. Only then do I roll back onto the road and pedal on toward the harsh yellow glow of the Port, still distant over the newly planted cornfields. Better not get killed. God knows, the coffee won't make itself.

When I was a kid, Asheville was still part of the Appalachians, though First Liftoff happened ten years before I was born and all the commercials for the new low-gravity suburbs were already exhorting us to *"Set aside your earthly treasures and experience life in the heavens!"* The flattening only started in earnest when I was in middle school. I'd see them passing us on the highway, when I could be bothered to look up from my gamepod—truckloads and truckloads of dirt and rock on their way to be oiled down and autopanned for usable minerals. That was all mountains were, really: mounds of dirt with things we could use inside them. The newly flat land was planted immediately with corn and soybeans.

"Look at that ugliness," Dad would say, spitting at the fields out the car window. "No more weather, no more variety. Just rows of rocket fuel."

I knew it was all right, though. They'd told us in school. Soon we would be living in *space*.

Not as soon as we thought, though. The house Mom bought to get away from Dad after I left for college is in a cheap little suburb, still on the ground but a few miles from the outer ring of strip malls and chain stores that grow out from the Cherokee Space Port like a fungus. It was an okay place to spend breaks that were never longer than two weeks. Mom seemed happy. The domed 'burbs were just a stopgap, built to shelter those of us who still had money from the angry folks who'd done the math and realized there wouldn't be room for everyone in low-earth orbit.

"Send us to Mars — We were meant for the Stars!" was the rallying cry my freshman year. I went to a few of the protests. Everybody did. Besides, I was half in love one of the organizers, a tiny girl named Leila who dressed in military jackets decorated with stickers and glitter and could stare down the private guards hired to patrol the science quad with the tense ferocity of a mother cat facing down an angry dog. But when finals came around, I quietly put away my cardboard signs and picked up my calculator. The number of general civs allowed low-grav immigration papers shrank every year: The first settlers had the money and power to keep it that way. Still, the number of engineers hired for corporate deepspace projects to find new planets and new fuel sources was growing exponentially. Junior year, I was in physics on the day of the Chapel Hill massacre.

I recognized Leila's bloody face in a news report on the victims. After that, my major stopped being my backup plan and became my escape plan.

"I need to get off this rock," I told mom when I was home for Christmas. She smiled the way moms do. Worried.

The summer I graduated, they closed out-of orbit immigration indefinitely. Deepspace funding was slashed. That's when the mass suicides happened.

I was not hired anywhere.

When I could leave the house again, I found a job in a little coffee chain in the Port that still did a brisk business with the rocketeers that shuttled back and forth carrying inanimate cargo, freight, and fuel to the low-gravity settlements above. I wore long sleeves to the interview, hoping to cover the newly healed scars on both my forearms. I shouldn't have worried; my new manager was much more concerned with my lack of transport. I cleaned off the old bike of dad's that had somehow ended up in mom's new garage among the slurry of boxes and other shit that had been mine or theirs and now didn't really belong to anyone anymore.

For the first few weeks, I dreaded my alarm. But my legs grew stronger. Now the long ride to work is the only part of my day I look forward to, the only time I can avoid thinking about the future.

I am just shifting back into flight when another honk breaks into my reverie. It's getting lighter now—almost proper daylight, if you were used to looking at it through a dirty basement window. Arching my neck around, I see a dim scowl and a baseball cap high above me in the red cab of another massive fuel tanker. The truck is already taking up eleven times more road than me, though at least this one slowed down. In all other directions, the road is empty.

He honks again. I hold up my middle finger.

Suddenly, my gravity is wrong. Time flipbooks. I see concrete and tires from above, like a bird, with no sense of what I'm watching. The right side of my body, face, ribs, and knee feel frozen, like I'm caught under an avalanche. My bike, me watching it, crashes to its side and skitters away backward through the truck's front wheels, disappears into the dark below. I wait my turn to be swallowed.

I am not swallowed. A pair of dirty brown boots approaches, crunching gravel. Then nothing.

I wake up in the truck, to the sound of a loud thump somewhere behind me. Looking out, I notice without comprehending that a man in a red hat is throwing a bicycle onto the open space between the cab of the truck and the tanker. I think about this for a little while. Then the door closes and the man is beside me, in the driver's seat

"Are you taking me to the hospital?" I ask. My voice comes from far away.

"No."

The engine starts. It occurs to me that I should be afraid.

The door opens and crashes shut, causing my head to jerk. The truck has stopped again. Or had it ever started?

Slowly raising myself onto my bleeding elbows, I look out the window. The man in the red hat is walking away from me, toward a big metal gate labeled "Private Property." The door handle wiggles uselessly under my hand—locked. I shake my head in an attempt to clear it. Bad idea. Through the spinning window, I watch the man fiddling with a padlock that hangs on one of those oversized chains looped through a stand of aluminum fencing, the kind of thing they put up around condemned buildings that have not yet succumbed to the terraformers. Behind the gate, some kind of short building, maybe an old gas station, boarded and graffitied into nothing more than a dark shed. The man in the red hat seems to have a screwdriver in his hand. He bangs it against the lock. The idea of his succeeding clears my head faster than felt possible a few seconds ago.

Get out, whispers every part of me. The door handle again. Still locked. Stretching my legs out into the drivers' seat, I can tell anyway that I'm in no state to run. Turning my numb neck back and forth, I stare for what might be a full minute before I recognize what I am seeing. My bicycle. In the back window, seemingly unbent. And a half-open window.

Pulling myself forward on my hands and my good right knee, I flop through the space between the seats and land half upside-down in the deep cavern behind the seats. It's dark, and God, I just want to curl up here and sob until someone comes to get me. Can't move.

Get out.

Reach up—one hand at a time, good girl, don't think—pull up. I hold both hands above my head like a diver and push with my feet against the drivers' side headrest, gasping at the sharp edge of the window which presses the air out of my chest. I bite down on a scream as my ribs scrape the window, then—thank God thank God for never having hips to speak of—I'm more than halfway through and gravity does its thing and I land on my back on top of the bike, which slides promptly sideways and almost dumps me the full ten feet to the ground. It had been tied to the back of the cab with a length of frayed shipping rope, which snaps when I hang from it with all the weight of my body. The frame is sound. The high cab of the truck looms over me, and as I swing a quickly-swelling knee over the middle bar I realize it's so massive that the bike fits neatly beneath the cab. He'd slowed down before the hit. Without the bicycle, there would be no evidence of the crash on the road.

Stifling a scream, I pedal just a few wobbly cycles. A horrible scraping noise. My stomach drops, then I look down and see the brakes locked tightly onto the wheel. I unhook them. A long gravel driveway leads away from the fence, and I pedal tentatively, trying to keep the body of the truck between me and the man. I'm at the head of the driveway before I hear the shout.

"Hey! Hey!"

At the end of the driveway is a stretch of main road, blessedly smooth. It's not hard to pick up momentum. I don't think for a second that I'm going to be able to outrun him along a flat like this—my only hope is to find somebody, anybody else, and flag them down. I stand all the way up on the pedals—my right knee screams—and pump along. The back of my throat hurts. A dull roar from behind me signals that the truck's engine has started again. *Damnit.* I didn't see his face. It's not fair. He should let me go.

Past the driveway, an unexpected fork takes me left, onto older-looking asphalt. Some quirk in the artificial landscape smooths and shifts, and I recognize rising before me the round top of the Hennessey hill. I'd cry if I could waste the time. I know where I am.

The old road that winds around the base of the hill meanders from the time when there were still creeks and forest stands and private property to avoid and meets up with the Port road very close to where the crash must have been. A newer road rolls up the hill and cuts back on itself halfway up where the slope was too steep for a straightaway, dead-ending at the base of the radio tower on the top—something to do with the Port, and the reason they spared the hill in the first place.

The reflective sign sparkles orange and white at the sharp turn above me: *DANGER!* Danger for cars. Danger for trucks. Only bicycles and rocket ships need apply.

Without bothering to look behind me, I pull right and begin the climb.

Almost immediately my legs and lungs burst into flames. It strikes me as odd that for my entire life I have called this beast a "hill"—a verbal tic, a callback maybe to thousands of years back when it was just a foothill in the shadows of its mountain family. Now it is the mountain, the oldest thing left in this strange, flat wasteland.

My legs are already bruised. Breath heaves out of me in big shuddering gasps. At the top of every cycle there is a sick, wobbling pause before I can force the pedal down again. To stop myself listening for the sound of the engine behind me, I begin to make promises.

I will live. Mom, Leila, I'm sorry. *I will live,* but not for any of the good reasons I should live for. Just because it seems like the most important thing in the world right now.

The unmistakable noise of a truck wafts up from behind me on the road.

I will live. My mind, detaching itself from my screaming body, notices the strata where the road makers sliced away the hillside—thick bands of history that formed themselves long before my ancestors climbed cautiously out of the treetops. *Sorry, Earth. I was just a kid.* But I'm not a kid anymore. Engines louder now—*shit.* Any second now....

I will live, and I'll do it on this planet that gave me life in the first place. The sentiment suddenly hits me, and I feel the prickle of tears at the side of my eyes. *I'll find a way.* It will never be what it was. Neither will we. But maybe this time, we'll be better. This rock's been shaped by greater forces than us. *I will live. I will stop running. I will change things for the better or go out trying.*

As if my promise has been heard and accepted, I reach the plateau next to the warning sign.

All I have to do is take my feet off the pedals, and it's as if I'd never been moving at all. My entire body trembles and aches. I finally allow myself to look back.

The roar of the engine had been deceptively loud. The truck is several lengths behind me, struggling with the weight of its load of fuel on the steep road. If he'd been thinking, he'd never have risked that thing up this slope. The sun behind me is blindingly pink, a full-on thin-aired mountain sunrise. The light is probably in his eyes. Good. Turning my bike, I launch myself down the hill straight into the path of the oncoming cab.

He swerves, then straightens out—seems to have decided to take me head on. I look into the glare on what should be the drivers' side and grin like a maniac. Then I lean right and flash past on the inside. I rocket into the dark between the tanker and the rock wall, howling with adrenaline. Then the light returns. The hillside passes by under my tires, turning faster and faster with no brakes to impede them.

Holy shit, I lived.

There is a screech and a crash, and in the corner of my eye I see a flash of red as the tanker, unable to turn in either direction, hits the barrier and keeps going. The fireball when it hits will be visible for miles. I can't think of it for more than a second. The ground flies past beneath me, and again I am an animal made of speed and wind, rolling faster and faster towards the turn at the hill's base.

I throw myself to the right. There is no crash, no noise other than wind. There is nothing other than this gravity that I am made for.

I fall and fall and fall until I am flying.

To See the Stars From Above

Jessie Kwak

When our wing buds had just begun to show through the backs of our shifts, Theo and I were taken with the other Hunter Aspirants to the Governors' Mission. It was a two-day journey to the coast—on foot, at least. Theo and I talked of nothing but how swift our return ride home would be along the hard-packed trails, when we would dodge cloying vines and send lizards scurrying.

We were meant to be bicycle Hunters, and had been cradled like the others of our caste in a chrysalis of banana leaves and silk from the golden orb spider. We had played at riding stick bicycles as children. We were ready.

The adults were barred from entering the Mission. They watched us go through the gates with set jaws and fearful eyes. Inside, we were made to stand in line while a squat Governor with furred cheekbones and silver talons examined the strength of our limbs and lungs, and opened our shifts to check the development of our wing buds. He growled happily over Theo's; mine he passed by without comment. Fear washed over me, but I needn't have worried. My name was called along with the seven others who were deemed worthy.

When we were led to the stables, Theo was not among us.

The Bicycle Master selected from among her herd of frames. For me, she chose a shy one from the far end of the stable. Even in its undressed form, before the Governors' workshop added its final components and weaponry, it was the most beautiful thing I had ever seen.

Some of the lower castes scoff that our bicycles are inanimate, but in the Hunter caste, we are taught that carbon is the building block of all life. And believe me, my bicycle frame flushed as gold as any newborn when I first took it under my palms.

We successful Aspirants rode home together in a wobbly pack—the unsuccessful were to follow us on foot. We would be in training by the time they arrived, and we understood we might not see them again for months.

⚙️

The Hunter caste was the most revered among the Tatoi, and I wore my armbands of golden orb spider silk with pride. We brought home meat, yes, but more than that we waged war on the Lesser Beasts, hunting them in our own humid jungle and out into the grassy plains they called home. I especially loved riding in the plains, catching a tail wind with my wings spread wide, as untethered as a ballooning spider.

Some of us excelled at speed, some at dexterity and tricks, some at accuracy of weapons. I excelled at silence; my prey heard the whirring of my hub only when I allowed it to.

I had a half-dozen kills before my training year was over. I was the youngest of my peers to have my ears notched and throat tattooed, and if I had not been ambushed one spring day I could have become the greatest Hunter of my generation.

Four of us were hunting that day. My companions lay in wait while I circled to the far side of the meadow, where a group of Lesser Beasts were foraging. It was a simple trap we'd used before. I approached in silence, then freewheeled near one of the younger females. At her warning the whole herd bolted, shouting to one another, with their young clutched to their chests.

I used the natural ramp of a buttressed root to turn, cutting sharply to chase down the female. She sprinted across a knot of roots—a common ploy—then flung herself over a clear patch of ground toward the jungle. Too late I realized the trap. My front wheel plummeted into the pit and I was thrown free, my feet wrenched from the clips.

I lay stunned a moment, winded, a searing pain in my left wing where the membrane had torn. When I opened my eyes, three spears pointed at my throat.

"We should kill her," a man's voice said. "We have the bicycle."

"Wait." A tattoo-faced, freakishly old Beast female squatted next to me, her white braids grown mossy, bark beginning to spread from her hairline.

I was repulsed. With that much bark growth, soon this Beast would begin to take root and die the slow painful death of her kind. If I had my weapon I would have killed her out of mercy.

"See how she looks at you, Nuana," said the first man. His spear dug into my throat. "She'd kill you if she had a chance."

I caught a startling scent and twisted my head toward the speaker. I found myself looking straight into the glassy wide-set eyes of a Tatoi man. More astonishingly, he had the tattooed necklace and ear notches of the Hunter caste.

This was not a Beast tribe. This was a splinter group of rebels. Fear thrilled through me.

The Beast female hauled herself back up, her woody limbs crackling with the effort. "We take her. You were young once, too, Yia."

They marched me with my hands tied behind my back, a specially-made netting harnessing my wings. My forearm throbbed, blood dripping from a dirt-filled gash. My torn left wing screamed with every step.

The disgraced bicycle hunter followed behind, his filthy hands guiding my bicycle. As far as I could tell, it was still ridable. The front wheel needed truing, and the right brake lever looked mangled but reparable. The firing mechanisms behind it were likely destroyed beyond my abilities to repair without the proper tools, however.

The rebels camped in the rocky hills above the plain. I had not known anyone lived there—it is where Beasts go to die. We marched through slopes covered with twisted, tortured-looking thorn trees that had once been alive, and the Beasts in the group touched their branches reverently. I looked away.

Other traitor Tatoi met us at the camp, their gossamer wings dull from malnutrition. Their ear notches indicated all number of castes, from Mechanics to Weavers to Nursery Workers. I saw no other Hunters, save myself and the disgraced man.

They tied me to a tree. If I craned my head, I could watch the other Hunter examine my bicycle along with one of the Mechanics. It remained lifeless under their hands as they straightened its bent handlebars and adjusted the derailleur.

As night fell, the old Beast female brought me food. I could not eat with my hands tied, and was at first too proud to let her help me. Hunger won over pride, eventually.

After a few bites, I tilted my chin at the bark at her hairline. "Doesn't that hurt?"

"My mehaiyu?"

"The bark."

"A little. But it's part of me."

"I thought it killed you Beasts."

Her tattooed eyebrows raised. "It transforms us. And yes, the transformation is painful. You Tatoi don't remember yours, as it happens at the beginning of your lives. But for the Manaru, it is at the end." She lifted her gaze to the branches above us. "This tree you're tied to, she is my aunt."

She smiled as I shuddered, revolted.

I was tied to the tree for three days. When the sun beat down on our dusty rock outcropping the Beast female, Nuana, brought me shade. When meals were cooked, she brought me food and helped me eat. When the sun was snuffed out for the night she brought me a blanket woven from rank-smelling wool.

On the morning of the fourth day, the disgraced bicycle Hunter, Yia, came to wake me.

I spat in the dust at his feet. "What've you done with my bicycle?"

"Repaired it."

"It belongs to me."

"It belongs to the Governors." The slits of his nostrils flared. "And so do you."

"I earned it!"

"Listen to yourself, girl." His wings rustled in irritation. "You've been nothing but a tool to the Governors, and the only reason you're still alive now is because you may still be a useful tool for us." His gaze flickered over and past me, to where I knew my bicycle was chained. Lust burned in his glassy eyes, but not for me.

I watched him walk away. Like a bird-spider watches her prey, I thought. Biding her time to leap.

That afternoon, Nuana put me to work. Washing and weaving, mostly. Nothing I could gain a weapon from. Nothing I couldn't do with my hands and feet still hobbled.

One of the other Tatoi, with the ear notches of a Nursery Worker, came to help. Something in the quirk of his jaw reminded me of Theo.

He asked the name of my tribe and told me his; he had come from nearer to the coast, where the Governors had first settled. "My grandfather was one of the first to see them," he said. "He was trading at a Manaru market when he saw their ship burning through the sky."

"Trading with the Beasts?" I laughed. "What would we want from them, twigs and moss?"

The man blinked slowly, the membrane clouding his glassy eyes. "They're skilled weavers," he said. He jutted his chin at my silk armbands, which gleamed in the bright sunlight. "They wove those. No matter how hard they try, we Tatoi still haven't learned how to milk golden orb spiders. I can tell your armbands are real, but since the wars began the Nurseries have had to dye worm silk yellow to swaddle Hunter larvae."

I shuddered. Worm silk? "You lie."

"It's an odd thing to lie about."

I plunged myself back into the washing. "I won't talk to a traitor." I could feel him watching me, but I refused to look up. After a moment, he unfolded himself and left.

I scrubbed furiously. What would be a worse truth: that Hunters today were swaddled in falsely dyed cloth, or that our grandparents had been swaddled in cloth woven by the same Beasts we hunted now? I stared at the band on my arm, remembering how proud I had been to take it, and how Theo—

Heavy footsteps approached, and I turned to see Nuana. "I think you've managed to clean that one," she said, and I stopped scrubbing, realizing how thoroughly I'd been working the same spot while I thought.

"I was remembering a friend," I said. "He didn't become a Hunter."

"I'm sorry," she said.

"Some of us pass the tests, some don't."

She tilted her head. In only the few days that I'd been here the bark had closed in another finger's width, curling in along the lines of her facial tattoos. She didn't have much time left to live.

Or, as Nuana had put it, she didn't have much time until her transformation. She had told me the day before that I was putting the old Beasts out of certain misery, but I had actually been denying them their true form. Like murdering a Tatoi larvae in its chrysalis, she had said. Obviously another lie, but— I shoved the sick feeling in my belly aside, and reached for another pot.

"Do you know what happens to those who do not pass?"

"They have lesser callings." I scrubbed. "I've been in training. I've not seen them to ask."

The beads in Nuana's mossy braids clacked as she sat beside me, taking up the Nursery Worker's scrubbing brush. "They never return. The Governors take our young back to their home planet—the Tatoi, especially. They value your wings and beauty. We Manaru they use in the mines and factories."

"That's not true."

"They give you the bicycles, the guns, the radios. What do you think you give them in return?"

"The Tatoi taught them to survive when they first landed here. The Governors are grateful."

"They're not grateful. They use you to hunt us, and they use us to distract you."

"That's not true," I said again. We finished the washing in silence.

That night, I looked into the stars, imagining Theo there in chains, his wings displayed for someone else's pleasure. If I had been less skilled, my legs shorter.... A thought struck me. The Governors had paid special attention to the development of our wings—hardly a trait needed for a skilled bicycle Hunter. I remembered the pleasure they had shown at Theo's.

I felt a chill, and pulled the musky blanket closer. What if I had been as beautiful as he? The stars twinkled overhead, cold and dead. The branches of Nuana's aunt's tree rustled, sending a single leaf to fall beside me.

❧

The next morning, when Nuana came to untie me, I turned to put my palms on her aunt's tree. I felt nothing.

"What do you want from me?" I asked.

Nuana looked at me slantwise. "We need weapons and strong riders, and we must act fast"

"You should have killed me. Yia can ride as well as I." Her words caught my attention. "Why must you act fast?"

"It's spring," she said simply.

Spring, when the Aspirants were marched to the Governors' Mission to imprint their bicycles. Spring, when those who failed were culled to serve among the stars. I shivered.

If I believed what this Lesser Beast was telling me...

That afternoon, Yia returned from his daily hunt early and empty-handed. He smelled of jungle, not the plains as he usually did, something the Lesser B—Manaru would never notice with their poor senses of smell. "I'll take the girl with me hunting tomorrow," he said to Nuana, ignoring me.

"I don't think she's ready."

Yia's wings shivered in annoyance. Or nerves. "I'll see that she's under guard. We don't have much time left, and there's new tech on her bicycle that I'm not familiar with. I need her to show me how to use it."

I could smell something else on him besides jungle. A faint scent from my childhood, salty and pungent and furred. Governors?

"She can show you here, Yia."

He turned his glassy eyes on me, his nostril slits pulsing once, then again. "Fine." He spun and stalked away.

I was woken before dawn when my blanket was torn off. Rough hands clamped over my mouth and ankles. I saw the glint of a knife, and the hobble at my ankles was cut. Yia crouched there, the bulk of his weight trapping my legs. Someone I could not see, though they smelled Tatoi, had one hand over my mouth while the other clamped onto my bound wrists.

"You're coming with us," Yia whispered. "Nuana will never give you your freedom, but if you help us I will. We must ride. You'll be silent?"

Ride? My heart thrilled at that, and I nodded. I didn't believe him in the slightest, but with unhobbled ankles and my bicycle.... His friend hauled me to my feet, jostling my torn wing. I bit back a yelp. I raised my hobbled hands to Yia. "Later," he said.

They supported me as I stumbled, my legs aching as I took real steps for the first time in a week. Yia unlocked my bicycle then mounted it, his fingers caressing the stem, trailing down the fork to check the tire pressure.

My bicycle was unresponsive beneath him. What had they done to it?

"Yia?" I tore my attention away from my lifeless bicycle to see Nuana. "What are you doing?" Her voice was loud, carrying. Behind her, the camp began to stir.

Yia's fingers inched toward the brake lever, to the row of weapons controls on the underside. Had he repaired them? His thumb brushed over the buttons, experimentally. Nuana did not notice.

"I already told you I was taking the girl out today," said Yia. He shifted, and I did, too. The Tatoi who held my shoulders had relaxed his grip, distracted. "I'll have her back by sundown."

"How long have you been hoping for this?" she asked softly. "Pretending to help, waiting for a chance to steal back to your masters?"

"They're not my masters." He yanked the front wheel to face her and I launched myself at him, my shoulder driving into his sternum. His shot went wild, flaring into the early morning air. We fell in a tangle of bodies and wings and bicycle, my torn left wing sending a nauseating wave of pain through me. I had landed on top, and I twisted, wrenching my upper body up to drive my elbow into his throat. Yia gurgled, then sucked for air as I planted both hands in his chest and pushed myself off him. I slashed my wrist hobble on my scythed front hub. He convulsed as I pulled my bicycle free.

It flushed gold and I felt giddy with relief. I turned its weaponry onto my other Tatoi abductor, who froze with hands raised. Behind him, the newly-gathered crowd shrunk back. I was nearly free. I almost laughed.

Only Nuana stood in my way, bleeding amber sap from her upper arm. She panted, nearly doubled from pain.

I tensed with one foot on the pedal, choosing my route so as not to strike her and injure her more.

"It's spring," she said softly, and stepped out of my path. She looked up to the sky. The last of the stars were fading as the sun rose.

I followed her gaze and felt a sudden vertigo as I imagined Theo viewing the stars from above, looking into an alien night sky to see our own home world twinkling impossibly far away.

I could chart a clear path past Nuana, but beyond that it became murky in my mind. Would I return to my tribe and continue to hunt the Manaru? Or would I confront my elders about secret yellow dye vats, the Governors, Theo?

"I need proof," I said.

Nuana nodded. "We can give you that."

"And the bicycle stays with me."

Nuana took an unsteady breath. "You'll forgive us if we don't entirely trust you."

"Likewise."

She laughed at that. "Put down your weapons, Hunter, and let's see if we can learn trust."

Overhead, the last of the stars was snuffed by the rising sun. I leaned my bicycle reverently against the tree that had been Nuana's aunt, then caressed the top tube. A trail of gold followed my fingertips. "Soon," I whispered, "we'll ride after a different sort of prey."

The gold pulsed. I turned back to Nuana.

"Tell me. I'll listen."

Kate Berube

The Kármán Line Brevet

Fritz Bogott

The Kármán Line—the near edge of outer space— is only 62 miles as the crow flies, but it's uphill all the way. You'll want to choose your route carefully.

The crow-flight route is theoretically possible, but you'll need to build or obtain a flagpole-climbing circus bike, and even the best ultracyclist could expect a maximum speed of around one meter per second. Even if you could sustain that pace for the entire 100km climb, it would take you 27 hours and change. I'm offering free pancakes for life to the first meathead who completes this route.

The most common (but still preposterously gnarly) route has a 10% constant grade, for a one-way distance of 1,005km. That's five 200km days in a row, each with a steep uphill grade all goddamn day. Hundreds of women and men complete this route each year.

There is some obvious good news about the 10% route: The return route is a cinch. If you wanted to, you could get home by smearing your body with chain grease and lying down.

The less obvious good news is the chow. You'll need to eat like a Norse giant just to maintain, and there are some truly excellent spots on the way.

If you follow the popular route from the foot of Market Street straight west-by-upwest, you'll encounter a long series of tethered, neutrally-buoyant and active-lift restaurants, coffee carts and snack stations catering to every taste and dietary niche. My old Army buddy Thura runs a soup balloon at kilometer 173 serving the best mohinga on or off-planet--but (no disrespect, man) the kicker is Thura's kids, who built themselves a little side-gondola from which they'll sell you a helmet-sized bucket of shrimp and vegetable fritters with chili sauce that will instantly restore your will to live. Don't miss it!

Curiouser and Curiouser

Lisa Sagrati

The rover trundled along the surface of the red planet. High winds had just wiped its solar panels clean, and it felt fresh and energetic. It was an elite robot with an important job to do. Its camera eye roved around. In the distance unearthly tall mountains loomed. Far to the north, a huge doughnut-shaped cloud hung over the horizon. Once, at the start of its working life, the rover had seen the larger of the planet's two moons traverse the sun.

Scanning the ground nearby, the rover spotted something unusual—a dark streak through the dust. This streak, the rover calculated, was narrower than its own wheels. Could a mini-dust devil have blown through? Its camera zoomed in for a closer look. There was something else odd about the track. It had a pattern to it—oblong shapes alternated left and right along its length. The rover's brain whirred, looking for similar images in its memory. Snakeskin? Stamp art? No—it most closely resembled a tire track. This must be the trace of a previous rover, one that had lost communication with Earth but continued to explore the planet. The rover's circuits thrilled in a semblance of excitement—perhaps it would meet its ancestor!

Its camera eye took the long view, following the trajectory of the track. It nearly had a processor attack—dozens of similar tracks striped the dusty surface up ahead. The rover quickly considered probabilities. Likelihood of a previous rover giving birth to a brood of baby rovers? Nil.

Likelihood of an alien civilization exploring the planet with a multitude of vehicles? Somewhat more probable.

But what seemed most likely (or, what the robot wanted to believe) was that it had finally discovered the long-sought biosignature—evidence of life on Mars. The tracks must be evidence of a snake-like creature, or one that moved on wheel-like appendages.

The rover summoned up its energy reserves and powered itself quickly—several centimeters per second faster than usual—toward the proliferation of tracks. After several hours it stumbled across an object half-buried in red dust. It reached out its forceps, grasped the object and lifted it carefully. It was paper thin, yet sturdy. The dust fell away and revealed the thing to be a shiny silver color. The forceps rotated and the camera saw garish colors on the other side. The rover placed the object into its chemical analysis compartment. Several minutes later, its synapses began to quiver in robotic excitement. Clumps of organic matter clung to the object!

The rover had been programmed to perform a dance of triumph upon its first confirmation of life on Mars. It now lurched clumsily in circles, waving its arm and neck in an imitation of joy. In fourteen minutes, scientists on Earth would receive the news and make their own dance-like motions. Celebration over, it got back to work.

Perhaps the organic matter was the scat of one of the creatures. But what was the shiny, colored, wrapper-like object? Toilet paper?

The rover planned its route—it would skirt the mass of tracks, careful not to disturb them. It lumbered along, noting with trembling circuits the varying patterns of tread among the tracks. These creatures left individual footprints.

The rover sighted and bee-lined for another stray object. It was a white cylinder of some tough but pliable material. Chemical analysis revealed it to be similar to plastic. Traces of organic matter remained in a palmate pattern on the cylinder and on the nozzle protruding from one end.

Continuing to track its quarry, the rover came upon a third object lying in the dust. It was a papery rectangle, white with large, black, symbol-like markings. Was this evidence of a literate culture? The rover conceded that the evidence most likely suggested a visitation from a sophisticated alien society rather than Martian life. The passage had been recent. The high winds on Mars would have erased any tracks left more than a few days ago. And yet the rover had registered no evidence of alien spacecraft. Were the creatures still here? The robot laid its camera head flat against the ground, feeling for vibrations. The planet was practically quaking in comparison to its usual stony stillness. Quick math revealed that the creatures, or their vehicles, were moving away at speeds approaching 20 kilometers per hour!

Entranced, the rover kept its head pressed to the ground. What speed these creatures possessed! What freedom, to be able to move so swiftly! It conceived an image of these lithe beings—they must be slim, streamlined, lightweight, elegant. It, Rover, had Brain, yes—but its mental agility was trapped within the confines of a graceless, elephantine frame. These creatures could cover more ground and see more of the strange planet in a day than the rover would in all its years.

The vibrations lessened, then stopped. The rover listened for a few more minutes, and then lifted its head. It was late in the day. Aiming its camera at the Martian sunset, it beheld a marvel—strange shapes silhouetted against the sun.

The rover understood. The creatures had taken flight and were heading off into the sunset. Its camera zoomed in and saw that each creature had two wheels. No—the creatures bestrode two-wheeled vehicles and moved their lower appendages rhythmically in circles to propel the vehicles. Their upper appendages gripped a bar at the front of their vehicles. The camera could not distinguish any facial features—either the creatures were wearing masks that allowed them to breathe in the Martian atmosphere, or their heads were machines like the rover's own. On their dorsal areas, each creature except one sported a white rectangle with black symbols. White cylinders were attached to the frames of the vehicles in various places. The rover spotted the hovering spacecraft the creatures were heading for. A portal opened and they disappeared inside, their Ride Across Mars complete.

Bipedal

Nicky Drayden

This isn't cheating, Dan'knor reassured herself as she spun the myriad of pedals on her octocycle, comforted by the familiar click of the complex network of eighty-eight gears. A buzz of nervous energy surrounded her, and she was ready to squirt a metaphorical ink cloud in the eyes of these unsuspecting humans. Dan'knor scanned the competition and their brightly colored swimwear that did little to offset the pallid color of their skin. She jutted her beak involuntarily. Not that she was the sort to flaunt her superiority, but her own waxy blue skin glistened luxuriously under the Earth's strange yellow sun. Nowhere in this triathlon's rulebook did it say that Octopodians were prohibited from entering the competition, an oversight on the humans' part. She'd gone over the "Participant Eligibility" section fourteen times, almost as many times as she'd gone over the section on "Awards" which specified that the winner would receive two hundred fifty dollars. With the pathetic intergalactic exchange rates, this was thirteen years' salary on her planet.

Dan'knor drew a deep breath and steadied her hearts. Now was no time to get her tentacles in a knot. There were a finite number of things expected from an Octopodian of her age. The primary (and most gracious) one was to slink into oblivion without so much as a grunt or a moan so that younger, smarter, more agile octopi could swim to the forefront. Dan'knor always resented this about her species. If she'd had the means, she would have shuttled off to the water world of Euri, where they knew how to treat their elders, but with the hit her retirement package had taken during the seventeen-year Octopodian hyper-recession, there was little chance of that happening. Heck, she hadn't even been able to afford the interstellar toll the entire way to Earth and had to spend the last 35 parsecs sledging through the fourth-class wormholes that were so dirty and greasy that not even filchlice would infest them.

"Next…" said a young human male with a dry, scratchy voice. His dull brown hair was done up in a mess of braided tendrils that reminded Dan'knor of the last brood she'd birthed, so many years ago now. "Name?" he said as Dan'knor stepped up to the registration booth.

"Dan'knor Jujer'bo'watkkzzz," Dan'knor said slowly but wetly, not giving into the temptation to use the humanized version of her name. At over three meters tall and with twice as many limbs as the rest of her competition, there was no way she wasn't going to stand out. Muting a few moist syllables wasn't going to change that.

The human male with the braided tendrils didn't even look up at her, just handed her a bib number, and then dismissed her with a lackluster "Next…"

At the start line, Dan'knor flushed from mantle to tentacle tips, eager to dive into the chilly water. These poor humans. She had seen how they "swam." It reminded Dan'knor of her childhood when they used to tie two eels together and watch them futilely wriggle and flail and fight. Sure, she herself was no great runner on land, but she was decent enough on her octocycle that if she pulled far enough ahead in this first swimming leg, she would win this thing tentacles down.

The horn sounded, and she was off. The cool waters slipped effortlessly past her taut skin. Muscles flexed, once, twice, and a final time, as she glided to the opposite shore. She didn't dare look back at the humans and their juvenile flip-flopping for fear of being consumed with laughter. Instead, she scanned the sea of bikes, looking for her own. It should have stood out as much as she stood out among the rest of the athletes, but it was nowhere to be found.

"Miss!" said a familiar scratchy voice. "Miss... Jooojuuurbooo..." the human male with the tendril hair came pedaling frantically towards her.

"Just call me Dan'knor," Dan'knor said testily. "Where is my octocycle? I'm wasting precious seconds here!"

"I'm afraid there's an issue, ma'am." The human male got off his bike and flipped his hair in a way that would have gotten him a punch to the beak in one of the rougher neighborhoods back home.

"I'm allowed to be here!" Dan'knor said. "There's nothing in the rulebook that excludes Octopodians from competing. It's not my fault I can swim so fast."

"So sorry. It's not that. I should have caught this earlier, but your...um...bike...it doesn't fit under the guidelines. In the rulebook, under the "Equipment" section, it says that bikes must be bipedal in nature, unlike your own."

Drat. Dan'knor cursed herself for skimming over that section.

"But here, you can use this bike!" He pushed his puny bicycle towards her. Dan'knor took a handlebar tentatively with one of her tentacles. She glanced back at the splashing mob nearly halfway across the lake, and then slung herself on the seat. The metal frame creaked under her weight. She slipped two of her tentacles into the toe straps, but felt odd not knowing where to place the others.

It took her four times as long as it usually did to build momentum, which she expected, but it surprised her how quickly her limbs grew tired despite how often she switched them out. She pumped as hard as she could and reached the next transition just seconds before her closest competitor.

The expanse of asphalt ahead of her made her stomachs sink. She slinked and slithered and slid, tentacles sticking to the ground, and the hot asphalt sticking to her. Runner after runner passed her until all she could see was the backs of hundreds of bobbing, furry heads. She cursed the intensity of this planet's strange yellow sun, and cursed herself for her stupid gamble. Now she'd be stuck on this sorry excuse for a planet without the fare to get back home. And from what she'd heard, the humans treated their elderly even worse than Octopodians did.

All was lost. Her slithering slowed and her slinking slunk.

"Come on, Dan'knor!" cried a scratchy voice from the crowd. Several more joined it, pleading with her to keep going. Complete strangers willed her on, and she pretended to hear the cheering and slurping of a few of her broodlings among them—Bru'Kphust, Cha'aair, and dear Bu'ulbb whose suckerflesh had once been nearly inseparable from Dan'knor's own. Despite herself, Dan'knor pushed on towards the finish line, and when she crossed it—had she shoulders, she would have felt the weight of the world lift from them. She'd done it. She'd finished a triathlon. The heaviness returned almost as quickly as it left as she saw the human male coming towards her, struggling to push her octocycle.

"You did amazing!" he said. "You finished!"

"I finished last," Dan'knor replied. "On my planet, the last place finisher becomes the celebratory meal for the first place finisher."

"Well, I guess it's a good thing we're not on your planet." The human male whipped his hair again, and Dan'knor had to refrain from scolding him. "Say, this is a pretty cool bike. Never seen anything like it."

Dan'knor let out a gurgle of offense. Who was this guy to tease her about her octocycle? Yes, it was a cheap, bottom-of-the-barrel clearance cycle from Splurtlemart, but it was the best she could afford. Just as she was about to tell him off, he offered to buy the bike from her.

"Forty bucks," he said with a straight face.

"What!" Dan'knor accidently let load of ink slip. Thankfully, it blended neatly into the black asphalt. "You've got to be kidding me!" Forty Earth dollars would get her back home, first class!

"Okay, Okay. One-fifty, but just so you know, I'll be eating ramen for the next month and a half."

Dan'knor growled and snapped her beak to the side of each of his cheeks to show her thanks for such generosity. The human recoiled, knees shaking so hard they knocked together.

"I'm sorry if my offer offended you," he spoke again, voice strained and two octaves higher than it had been before. "Three hundred dollars, that's really the best I can do."

"Deal!" Dan'knor struck out four of her tentacles, and closed them around the human male's sweaty palm. Three hundred Earth dollars? She was rich beyond her wildest dreams! She could travel to Euri and live out the rest of her life in luxury. "Thank you so much, human male."

"You can call me Zeke."

Dan'knor shuddered at the obscenity. Who in their right mind would name their child after such a horrid act of gangliary eroticism? She shook her head. They were merely humans. Simple creatures, still bumbling their way up the evolutionary ladder. Dan'knor reached out and smoothed down his tendrils, reminiscing about the fondest of her broodlings...Jym'bahg, Bal'aae, and sweet Tra'vul who'd been the last to stop visiting home on High Quenching Day. But this human male and his wet-heartedness reminded Dan'knor the most of her very favorite. "If it is okay, I would prefer to call you...Lu'unch," she said, giving in to the urge to wrap him up tightly in her suckerflesh, and taking comfort in the subtle trembling of his body.

Nova's Cycles

Aaron M. Wilson

I nez Wick sat in the public library at a computer. Her bobbed electric blue hair was pulled back out of her eyes with bright yellow barrettes made from bicycle chain links. It was hot, and she wore a white tank top that bared her arms, which were covered in tattooed green vines with purple and pink flowers. Despite the airy attire, she was sweating, and her eyes were beginning to droop as she scanned the employment listings. The ad headings were beginning to blur when she spotted one that woke her right up.

Wanted: Experienced Bicycle Mechanic. Relocation is a Must. Adventurous. Single. No Family Ties. Serious Inquiries Only. Nova's Cycles.

Curious, Inez keyed in a search. Only one entry turned up—an article featuring a picture of a woman holding a single speed bike with balloon tires over her head in front of a small, junky looking space freighter. The side of the ship said, "Nova's Cycles," in block lettering, and the 'o' in Nova was replaced with a chain ring.

The article was about a project to take bikes to the colonies. Nova's first stop would be the moon, with aspirations to reach the frontier. She was quoted as saying, "Bikes represent freedom of mobility, and the colonies are in sore need of a little bit of freedom." The quote was the kind of dangerous political slip that got Inez excited. Surely, she was referring to the rumblings of separation that trickled through the news filters set in place to keep what was really going on in space from reaching the masses on earth, even though most people knew something was amiss in space.

Inez looked up from the screen and took a long draw from her now cold coffee. *Bikes in space, freedom for the colonies*, she thought, *I need to meet this Nova.* Inez had worked in shops for several tune-up seasons as she drifted around the Midwest. She had been asked on several occasions to stay on as a regular mechanic, but her true passion of environmental monkey business kept her on the run. As of late, she had run out of places to hide, so space had a certain appeal.

⚡

Two weeks later, Inez was working on the bottom bracket of an abused cargo bike. She had just finished cleaning and greasing. Now, she was spinning the crank opposite her wrench, reattaching it and tightening it down.

Nova pushed off the wall at one end of the servicing area and landed at the other end next to Inez. They both wore identical blue overalls specially made for working in low gravity. Instead of cargo pockets on the legs, arms, and abdomen, those sections were loaded with ball bearings, packed tightly to form flexible, magnetic plates under the cloth. Nova plucked a cone wrench from Inez's left leg and put it back on the magnetic tool wall.

"Try to keep the tools that you're not using where they belong. It only takes a second to put it back after you're done." She pulled two more wrenches off of Inez's uniform and put them back. "Just one loose tool…"

Finishing Nova's speech, Inez said, "and boom!" She wiped the excess grease off the bike she was servicing and tucking the dirty rag into her pocket.

Together, they took the bike off the work stand and put it with the others they were readying for sale. It took two people to unbuckle the bikes and secure them. Thus far, Nova had put together twenty new fat tire snow bikes, which she felt would translate well to the dusty and rocky surface of the moon. Meanwhile, Inez had been given the dirty work of salvaging the used bikes that were piled high in one of the storage bays. To Nova's twenty, Inez had successfully built up five bikes.

Nova said, "That's a fine looking cargo bike. You even found racks for over the front wheel." She griped Inez's shoulder firmly. "You're a real magic worker."

"Your parts piles," Inez grimaced, "have seen better days." She held up a chain ring. The teeth had a shark tooth curves instead of sharp triangular points. She placed it into a large bucket. "Pure scrap."

Nova shook her head. "I didn't have time to check the lot over. How many bikes do you think are in those piles?"

"Hard to say." She wiped chain grease across her forehead. "I'll know more when I can see the back wall."

🚲

The moon was a bust.

Nova had parked in the market district between a vendor of stuffed animals and a clothing re-seller. The market was just outside the atmospheric bubble where families lived and spent most of their time. Vendors like Nova's Cycles landed and parked there, paying a hefty docking fee. Then on market days the docking seal opened so that shoppers could walk into the mobile shops.

Since there were no bikes on the moon, there was nothing to fix, so Inez spent the better part of her day riding around the settlement, a four mile by four mile bubble, on one of Nova's balloon-tired snow bikes, putting up flyers and showing off her skills to young boys and girls.

After a few days of this showing off, the shop started to see a lot of foot traffic... but still no sales. It seemed that everyone was saving to get off the moon and return to earth. The miners made good money in theory, but the cost of their uniforms, equipment, housing, electricity, waste removal, water, and even air was deducted directly from their paychecks. What was left over did not amount to much.

Nova, however, was not about to give up her dream. She held a free raffle and gave away two used bikes and one new one, which were happily accepted by the winners. She and Inez watched as each proud new bike owner rode away.

They sat together on the ramp up to the shop door. Artificial day turned into twilight. A boy wearing a slouching knit cap steeped up and put a small white box of leaflets into Nova's hands. He touched his index finger to his nose before disappearing.

Inez's eyebrow rose inquisitively.

"Not here."

Without even one sale, Nova gave the order to pack up the shop, and they left for Io.

🚲

Days later, the orders started to roll into Nova's Cycles' website. By the time they landed on Io six months later, everything they had in stock was spoken for and Inez was busy building up more used bikes.

Inez had asked about the box. She had even searched for it. The box was not in the shop, the kitchen, bathroom, the cockpit, or the engine room. After docking on Io, however, Nova handed the box to Inez along with an address.

"So," Inez asked, "are you going to tell me what this is all about?"

Nova looked around the shop and smiled. "You'll get your answers when you deliver that package." She put her hand on Inez's shoulder and looked into Inez's eyes. "I know who you are, the real you. The you that is wanted for domestic terrorism..."

"Eco..." Inez shook off Nova's grip.

Nova put her hands in the pockets of her shop apron. "Whatever. It's why I hired you." She looked around the shop again and shook her head. "Just deliver the package, and you'll get your answers." Nova walked past Inez and opened the large garage door. The compressed air of the ship popped and equalized with the colony.

Inez dumped the box into a bag and slung the bag over her head and across her chest. She saluted Nova before picking out a full suspension mountain bike she had just finished the night before they landed, and rode off.

⚙⚙

The people of Io had it worse than those on the moon by the look of things. The streets were covered in dust. The domiciles were thick with crumbling red-brown rust. The atmosphere in the dome was think and difficult to breath. Inez had to downshift and slow her breathing to keep from hyperventilating. But the worst symptom of despair was that not a single soul was out on the streets. Io, to Inez's eyes, was a ghost town.

The address was a small unit with a green door, identical to all the other units on the block. It had two steps up to the door, a small round window off to the left, and mail box to the right. Just like all of the others this home was also covered in thick rust that flaked off when Inez rang the bell.

The door opened. A man in Io issue overalls and bare feet stuck out his hand. "Welcome, Inez. I think that you have something for me." He stood to the side of the door and ushered her inside.

The inside of the home did not seem to fit with the outside. The furniture was in good shape. The walls were painted a deep red. The floor was covered in a richly textured yellow carpet. Pictures of friends and family hung on the walls.

"Have a seat." The man ran his thick hands over his shaven head. He kept talking while Inez found her way to a wooden chair. "Nova needs to be sure about you, so she sent you to me. I realize that this is all going to seem like back story to your future in a couple of minutes, but the we have to be careful."

"We?"

"Yes. Nova and I are separatists; well, not separatists, not really. We want rights, representation, not just for the

Moon and Io, but for all of the colonies." He held out his hand. "Can I see the package?"

Inez dug it out of her bag and handed it over. "What does this have to do with me?"

He opened the box and removed a few of the leaflets producing a smaller package that he handed back to Inez. "You have a skill set that we need."

Inez slowly turned the package over in her hands. It was a tiny plastic orb containing a gel that bounced and shimmered. Inez closed the box and looked up.

"It is your tool of choice, correct?" He cracked a toothy grin. "We need you to start a war. Your track record is immaculate, no human casualties. We want to act but we cannot take first blood."

Inez looked at the ground. "You're wrong. The coal plant in China…" She stopped mid sentence. To be honest, she had been looking for a new cause. Earth, though not yet the ecological nirvana she envisioned, had fixed most of the environmental problems she had been fighting to solve.

She turned back to face her host. "So, what do you want me to blow up?"

❧

Io, like the moon, had been an initial bust. Not one bicycle sold. Yet, once again, a few days en route back to the lunar dome, a flood of orders for mostly used bikes appeared.

"Nova," Inez asked, "are these orders bogus, a cover?" Inez did not look up from the road bike she was rigging with caliper brakes. With plastic ties, she secured the brake cord housing along the frame.

"When I took on this project," Nova winked, "I didn't expect to sell anything. The plan was to create false orders, but I guess there is no need."

"Good." Inez trimmed the break cord and tested the rear. The calipers brought the thin road bike wheel to quick stand still. "This is the one." She stood up and looked over the bike. "It's light, in good shape, and has the housing space in the tubing that I'll need."

Nova nodded.

"What's your plan for after?" Inez continued to circle the completed road bike.

"We have orders to fill." Nova put a serious emphasis on orders. "I'll wait a week before returning to space. Will that give you enough time to make it back?"

"It should, as long as my past does not catch up to me earth-side."

&bike;

Inez had not expected to be Earthside so soon, but she reveled in the sun on her skin and the uncirculated air in her lungs as she rode one of the bikes she had built up, special, on the return trip.

The address that she was given on Io was for an expensive looking home on a beautiful street with once-manicured lawns and tall shade trees. The street should have been filled with happy children chasing an ice cream truck, or at the very least, joggers and bicyclists. Instead, the neighborhood was completely uninhabited. It was an investment venture that had soured, she'd been told, owned by the umbrella company that managed the Io and Moon workers' contracts. This first strike was only supposed to be symbolic—no lives taken.

Inez locked the bike to the trunk of a newly planted apple tree with heavy chain. She dropped the silicone capsule into a small hole she had drilled into the frame. She looked at her watch and started a timer for thirty minutes. The walk back to where she had stashed her other ride was twenty-five minutes, plenty of time.

Inez pedaled hard. With only minutes remaining, she felt confident in her work and her ability to make it back to Nova's Cycles. The spaceport was only a day's ride. However, she had to watch. She pulled off the road and leaned against a tree. Seconds later, the explosion rocked the ground under her feet. It was followed by a series of smaller pops, which were the individual houses going up like popcorn. Inez had studied the plans for the community long and hard. Underneath the apple tree, where she had locked the bike, had run a major gas line.

Inez smiled at a job well done. Quickly, she got back on the road with smoke and fire behind her. She needed to get back to Nova's Cycles. She had more bikes to restore if they were going to fill all the orders that, she was convinced, would start the real revolution.

The Revelation of Megulon-5

I know what you're thinking when you roll up here. You're thinking about the future. You're thinking that something kinetic is going to happen. The roads will buckle and heave, the gas stations will spew flaming geysers. The bridges and tunnels will be choked with the bodies of cars suddenly maladapted to an environment no longer tailored to them, and in those cars the bodies of the people, also dead in an environment that can no longer keep them alive, no AC and no way to fill their empty cup holders.

I know what you're thinking because everyone thinks the same thing, always. We can't stop thinking about it. It is the curse of Prometheus. It is not the talons of the eagle which we fear the most, it is the sound of the approaching wings.

And you know what I'm going to tell you. You don't even have to listen to me, because it's something you've been told over and over by your entire world. You know it already. You know that you're peering through a miasma of fear and dread. You believe it comes out of the machines all around you, but in fact you are exhaling it out of your own mouth. You're worried about the heavens and the hells in front of your handlebars. You see the grinning maw and you think your little life is going to change. You think that the future is before you, and the past is behind you, but it isn't. You're not rolling forward. You're there already, and you're already long gone.

What I'm telling you is that you're suffering because you're ignorant. Your tender ass is clenching because you don't know any better. You think something happened, or is going to happen, but you don't realize that it's happening this very instant, always. And this is important, because you've been looking forward to the end of the world. You think that among the tribulations you will wheel, alive, and more importantly, free. There will be the wailing and the gnashing of teeth and above it all, you, look, no hands! Make way, chumps, gotta get these toys to the children! But listen! The time to be a hero is past! You're already drowning in the banal swamp of the damned, and you're already singing with the moronic choir. The apocalypse happened and you don't even know about it.

Listen. Let me tell you how I know this. I know it because I was once as idiotic as you are, but I thought I was clever. I thought I could bring about the end of my world by throwing the old one away. I thought that I could renounce intelligence and wisdom, renounce my motivation and understanding. And I did, to a point. I defied gravity and momentum. I invented a world where these concepts didn't apply. I took my bike apart and put it back together while I was riding it. I rode headlong into my friends. I skitched a bus and left a stain on a police car. I catapulted my body into the air. I rode backwards, sideways, inside out. I sustained head injuries, I developed a rash. And I was free! I knew that gravity, friction, and inertia were only voices inside my head, and I was able to ignore them as easily as I disdained the laws of man. I poked my head through the end of the world and the sky, and found a bubble of utopia that kept me alive in the lake of shit. I threw off my chains. And you can do it too! But listen! It will not work! There is one thing I could not relinquish, and that was the wheel! I thought I could unmoor myself from this bay of floaters, and I almost did. But I could not escape the wheel! My feet still spin, my heart still pumps, and my mind still races, rolling away and back, always rolling back. Always giving me direction and velocity! Always establishing a location and a destination!

Listen! I know what you're thinking because I know what you are! You're a messenger, and I know what you're delivering, and you don't. You think you're bringing something from here to there - a word, a feeling, a presence, a witnessing. But you're wrong! You're bringing there to here. You're bringing then to now. You are not on the wheel, or even in the wheel, you are of the wheel. And the wheel is what matters. You need not concern yourself with the flesh of civilization; it will slough off around you. You are raising the painted backdrop yourself. Your hands are setting up the props right before you turn your head to view them. So how do you roll? Do you roll as if the buildings are falling down around you? Because they are! Do you roll as if you are on fire? Because you are! But you are not consumed! You will not need to duck and cover. You only need to keep your eyes on the road so you will know where you want to put it! Listen! This is your only chance! It is the last day! Do you doubt I know what I'm talking about? Do you think you're ready to prove me wrong?

The Breathing Engine
Matthew Lambert

I'm a professional cyclist. Every morning the shuttle takes me to the power plant and I pump my legs to crank the turbines. My Gran said it didn't used to be like this; they used to burn coal and petrol, pumped out of the ground and into the fire, through the wires to cozy little homes. But now the sky is dark with dead dinosaur breath, and the cozy homes have airtight windows.

She had so many stories about biking outside. Down roads and mountains, across bridges. Wind in your hair, offering you flower smells. Lungs heaving, panting, pulling in air to power her legs. She used to breathe so deep. But the air got worse and worse, and eventually that had to stop. She was old, and the smog was hard on her lungs. She couldn't take deep breaths; couldn't ride outside anymore. So she brought her bike to a little power plant co-op, popped off the wheels, put it on blocks, and geared it to the old turbine. Back then the co-op just powered an air purifier. "The next best thing to biking outside, she said, "is biking so other people can." And then the petrol ran out, and the solar panels couldn't see the sun through the soot. The little co-op got really, really big: they brought in bikes from the landfills and bums from off the streets. There isn't any money in air purification, so that had to go. Now it's just kilowatt hours; as many as they can squeeze out of us.

They gave us virtual reality glasses to improve "employee satisfaction." Because let's face it, spending eight hours a day staring at your coworker's sweaty backside isn't exactly inspirational. A lot of people use them to check their email, some watch movies...I'm pretty sure some of the guys are just looking at porn. I bike. Like Gran used to. Outside. It's amazing. Roads lined with green, sprawling trees. Flowers of every color and size. Hills, up and down, meandering curves, bright yellow sunshine. And in my ears the sounds of birds, the rushing of the wind, the popping of rocks underneath my tires. And when I concentrate, I can almost feel the wind: the sting of it hitting my eyes, the thrill of it tousling my hair, whipping around me in a cool cocoon. Breathe deep.

I was working my way up a huge, grassy hill toward a beautiful pine tree, when the tree, the hill, and the grass all disappeared. There was just Paul's bent back, and a message in my glasses:

ATTN: VR Trial Period: Week One.
When we distributed the VR glasses, we hoped they would make you happier and more productive. However, our overall energy production is down. Please remember the VR is a tool to increase your motivation and productivity; use it as such.

My pine tree was back. For now.

During my cool down hour I installed a bigger gear on my front sprocket to get more power and asked my glasses to give me more challenging terrain in the simulation. Rougher roads, bigger ups, fewer downs.

And yet the next week my babbling brook was swallowed up by Paul's back and more foreboding text:

But the numbers were worse the next week, in spite of my efforts to persuade my co-workers to try the outdoor simulation. Or to just, you know, do their fucking jobs. I tried to be good about the switch back. I really did. But the pines, rivers, hills, birds, and flowers I could not name were gone, and in their place was Paul's sweaty, heaving back, legs flying round and round, going nowhere fast. I kept hearing Gran's stories in my head, and I wanted to have my own.

So I ventured into the attic to find Gran's old bike stuff, in a box in a corner covered in dust. Tools, a pump, a book, and best of all, wheels: shining, silver wheels. I polished them 'til they shone like hospital tools. I inflated the tires slowly; triple checked the pressure.

The next day I showed up to work with Gran's precious bike wheels and a gas mask.

It took a long time to fix Gran's bike. I couldn't figure out how to get the wheels past the brakes, at first. And I had to detach it from the turbine and thread the chain onto the back gears.

By the time I was done my hands were covered in grease and small scratches. And then I realized I'd never learned how to ride a bike. Properly, I mean. With balance and stuff. So I wobbled down the locker room hall, and wobbled back, arm against the wall for balance. Eventually I got the hang of it, and everyone stared as I emerged from the hall and rolled towards the airlock. I pulled on the gas mask. The turbine droned on, unfazed.

Now I'm standing in the airlock, looking through fish-eye lenses, and wondering if it's worth it after all. I might not even make it home. I strain my lungs with a deep breath and push the button. The door hisses as the grey air blasts in and curls up next to the rear door. I mount Gran's bike and pedal outside.

It's not like the VR. And it's not like Gran's stories. Even through the gas mask's carbon filters, the air smells smoky, metallic, and old. There are no birds, and their trees are withered. The sun looks faint and far away, and its warmth on my hands is feeble. I make my way down to the riverside trail; it was Gran's favorite. I start pedaling in earnest, trying to keep up with her ghost. My legs circle under me as I rush forward, bouncing up and down with the cracks in the road, the dusty air whipping through my hair. Leaning side to side through graceful turns as the river meanders beside me.

I can almost hear Gran's laugh, and I laugh with her. The dinosaur breath is starting to sneak through the carbon filters and into my heaving lungs. But I have never felt so alive.

Contributors

Amelia Greenhall is a designer and data scientist in San Francisco. She's into bike touring, quantified self, cooking, writing, and making things: ameliagreenhall.com

Maddy Engelfried is a college student in Portland, Oregon who uses her powers for good.

Elizabeth Buchanan writes and thinks about the end of the world more than is probably healthy. She lives in Austin, Texas with a boycat named Esther and occasionally posts things at www.goes-the-weasel.com

Jessie Kwak is a freelance writer who lives in Seattle amongst towering stacks of books, fabric, and bicycles. She blogs about bikes and crafts at Bicitoro.com, and you can also find her on Twitter (@ JKwak).

Kate Berube is the author of *Hannah & Sugar* (Abrams) and the illustrator of *The Summer Nick Taught His Cats to Read* (Simon & Schuster), You can find Kate's prints, greeting cards, and more at kateberube.etsy.com She lives in Portland, OR.

Fritz Bogott (fritzbogott.com, @fritzbogott) writes tall tales and rides his dad's forty-year-old Raleigh touring bike in Northfield, Minnesota.

Lisa Sagrati lives in Portland, Oregon, where she writes, bikes short distances slowly, and builds her qi. Her first contribution to *Taking the Lane* appeared in the "Bikesexuality" issue.

Nicky Drayden is a Systems Analyst who dabbles in prose when she's not buried in code. She resides in Austin, Texas where being weird is highly encouraged, if not required. She's the author of over 30 published short stories and her debut novel *The Prey of Gods*, a near future thriller set in South Africa, is available from Harper Voyager, Summer 2017.

Aaron M. Wilson is notably a writer of short stories. His fiction is a strange mixture of science fiction, urban fantasy, bike mechanics, tattoos, yoga, and environmental activism. When he is not staring off into the void, cooking dinner, doing laundry, or running after his rainbow attired daughter, he enjoys contemplating whether Fox Mulder and Dana Scully would rather join the Justice League or Avengers.

Megulon-5 is a founder of C.H.U.N.K. 666, a mutant bicycle club and civic society preparing for an apocalyptic adjustment in the physical and psychological urban environment. He publishes their achievements at dclxvi.org/chunk.

Matthew Lambert is an author and biker. He loves stories in all their forms, and particularly enjoys writing flash fiction. He can be reached at isanyonereadingthis@gmail.com

SUBSCRIBE TO EVERYTHING WE PUBLISH!

Do you love what Microcosm publishes?

Do you want us to publish more great stuff?

Would you like to receive each new title as it's published?

Subscribe as a BFF to our new titles and we'll mail them all to you as they are released!

$10-30/mo, pay what you can afford. Include your t-shirt size and your birthday for a possible surprise!

microcosmpublishing.com/bff

...AND HELP US GROW YOUR SMALL WORLD!